Three Little Kittens

First published in the United States by
Ideals Publishing Corporation
Nashville, Tennessee 37214

by arrangement with
Michael O'Mara Books
London, England

Designed by Simon Bell

Printed and bound in Belgium by
Proost International Book Production

Library of Congress Cataloging-in-Publication Data

Smith, Linda Jane, 1962–
  Three little kittens / Linda Jane Smith.
    p.   cm.
    Summary: Despite their mother's warnings, Barney leads his two
sister kittens over the garden wall into a scary overnight adventure
in the alleys.
    ISBN 0-8249-8490-0
    [1. Cats—Fiction.]   I. Title.
PZ7.S6543Th   1990
[E]—dc20   90-5102
                                                  CIP
                                                   AC

Three Little Kittens

Linda Jane Smith

IDEALS CHILDREN'S BOOKS
Nashville, Tennessee

Barney and Suki are very happy cats. They have three little kittens: Yaki, who looks just like her mother; Little Barney, who looks just like his dad; and Rolly, who looks a little like both parents.

Little Barney is a chip off the old block. He wants to be just like his dad when he grows up. Nearly every day, Little Barney says, "Please, Dad, tell me about the time when you were an alley cat."

"In those days a cat had to stand on his own four feet," Big Barney always says, puffing out his chest. "I lived in a cardboard box with nine other cats but I caught enough mice each day to keep us all fat."

"I'm sure I could catch a mouse," thinks Little Barney, "if I ever saw one."

8

One day, Suki was reading a story to the three kittens. The story was about a kitten who got lost. The poor little kitten was chased by a big, one-eyed tomcat, fell in a pond, and had all sorts of terrible adventures.

"Why are you telling us such a scary story, Mommy?" asked Yaki.

"I just want you to know that the rest of the world is not as safe and cozy as our house. You must be very careful—and never, ever climb over the garden wall."

But Little Barney was not listening. He was thinking, I'll bet there are lots of mice on the other side of that wall. If I went over and caught some, Dad would be very proud of me.

Later, Little Barney told Yaki and Rolly about his plan.

"It won't take long," he said. "There are lots of mice out there, and all we have to do is gather them up."

"But Mommy warned us not to climb over the garden wall," said Rolly.

"All mommies talk like that," said Little Barney. "Just think of how happy she will be when we bring back lots of fresh mice for dinner."

11

"But what about all the scary things out there, like big, one-eyed tomcats?" asked Yaki.

"If we see anything scary, all we have to do is hop back over the wall. What could be easier than that?" answered Little Barney.

He climbed onto some pots and leaped to the top of the wall.

"Come on! I'll help you," he shouted.

"I suppose it will be all right for a few minutes," said Rolly.

"Yes, and we'll have fresh mice for dinner," added Yaki, licking her lips.

13

14

When they had dropped down on the other side of the wall, they all looked up.

"That's funny," said Little Barney. "The wall seems a lot higher from this side."

"How will we ever get back?" Yaki said in a very soft voice.

"We can worry about that later, after we've caught lots of mice," answered Little Barney.

Just then, a very big mouse who was hopping across a trash can knocked some cans to the ground with a great crash.

"It's a dog!" cried Rolly.

"It's the tomcat!" cried Yaki.

"Run for it!" cried Little Barney, and they all scampered off in different directions.

17

They ran and ran until they were completely lost. When Yaki and Rolly stopped running, they couldn't see Little Barney anywhere.

"Barney! Barney! Barney!" they shouted, thinking that they would never see him again.

But a few minutes later, Little Barney appeared. He looked just as frightened as Yaki and Rolly.

"It's getting awfully dark," he said, pulling his sister and brother close to him under the light of a lamppost.

"Y-yes," whispered Rolly, "and I think there is something out there."

The poor little kittens spent the whole night huddled together. They heard lots of scary noises, but they kept their eyes shut tightly and thought about their mommy and daddy and their nice, warm beds at home.

In the morning, they were cold and hungry.

"I'll catch some mice," said Little Barney. "That will cheer us up."

There were lots of mice around, and Little Barney ran all over the alley after them, jumping in and out of trash cans and getting himself into a terrible mess.

"You said we could catch lots of mice in only a few minutes," cried Yaki, "but we've been here for ages and you haven't caught one little mouse."

"I guess the mice must be faster now than they were when Daddy was a kitten," said Little Barney. "But Dad said that he used to find lots of good things in trash cans when he was an alley cat," he added and leaped onto a trash can, which fell with a crash to the ground.

This was a big mistake, for inside the can was a big, scary, one-eyed tomcat.

"Oh no, it's the tomcat!" cried Yaki and Rolly.

"Run for it!" shouted Little Barney, and they all raced away.

23

Barney and Suki had been searching all night and all day for their three little kittens.

"My poor babies," said Suki. "They must be cold and hungry and frightened. Why did they ever climb over the garden wall? I told them how dangerous it is out here."

"It's all my fault," said Barney. "I have often told Little Barney of the adventures I had when I was an alley cat. I think he is just trying to be like his dad."

The poor little kittens had a terrible day. They chased after mice but couldn't catch any, and the big, one-eyed tomcat chased them all over the alleys. They tried to find their way home but all of the alleys looked the same.

"We've walked for miles and I'm hungry and it's getting dark again," wailed Rolly. "What are we going to do?"

"We are lost forever," sobbed Yaki.

"We have to find a place to sleep tonight," said Little Barney, bravely. "If we are going to be alley cats, we must make an alley cat's bed."

After a while they found a box filled with old newspapers.

"This will do," said Little Barney, and they all settled down to sleep.

28

They were fast asleep when Yaki heard a voice. Tapping her two brothers with a paw, she whispered, "There's someone out there in the dark."

The three little kittens peered out into the darkness, but all they could see were four big eyes.

"Oh no," cried Rolly. "It's *four* one-eyed tomcats!"

"No it isn't," shouted Little Barney. "It's Mommy and Daddy!"

"We're saved, we're saved!" yelled Rolly and Yaki.

They all hugged and kissed one another again and again.

"You must all promise never to climb over the garden wall again until you are grown-up," said Suki.

"We promise," said Yaki and Rolly.

"And what about you, young fellow?" asked Barney.

"Oh, I guess I promise, too," answered Little Barney with a shrug.

The three little kittens had a great big meal, and then Barney lit a warm fire.

"Daddy," asked Little Barney, "how did you catch all those mice when you were young?"

"Barney, don't you dare answer that question," cried Suki.

Big Barney laughed. "No more adventure stories for you, Little Barney." And they all cuddled up in front of the fire.